Baby Face

A Book of Love for Baby

Cynthia Rylant   Illustrated by Diane Goode

A Paula Wiseman Book
Simon & Schuster Books for Young Readers
New York London Toronto Sydney

SIMON & SCHUSTER BOOKS FOR YOUNG READERS

An imprint of Simon & Schuster Children's Publishing Division

1230 Avenue of the Americas, New York, New York 10020

Text copyright © 2008 by Cynthia Rylant

Illustrations copyright © 2008 by Diane Goode

SIMON & SCHUSTER BOOKS FOR YOUNG READERS is a trademark of Simon & Schuster, Inc.

Book design by Einav Aviram

The text for this book is set in Bembo Infant.

The illustrations for this book are rendered in pencil, watercolor, and gouache.

Manufactured in China

10 9 8 7 6 5 4 3 2 1

Library of Congress Cataloging-in-Publication Data

Rylant, Cynthia.

Baby face : a book of love for baby / Cynthia Rylant ; Illustrated by Diane Goode.

p. cm.

ISBN-13: 978-1-4169-4909-1 (hardcover)

ISBN-10: 1-4169-4909-7 (hardcover)

1. Infants—Juvenile poetry. 2. Children's poetry, American. I. Title.

PS3568.Y55B33 2008

811'.54—dc22

2007015817

For Peter—D. G.

Baby Face

A tiny nose,
a tiny mouth,
a tiny pair of ears.
Two big eyes,
a bit of hair,
a little bit of tears.

Smile for me, sweet baby face.
Make the whole world shine.
Let me see your baby face.
Tell me you are mine.

A perfect nose,
a perfect mouth,
and extraspecial ears.
I love those eyes,
I love that hair,
I love those no-more-tears.

Baby lovely,
Baby sweet,
Baby so divine.

I love your pretty baby face.
Tell me you are mine.

Baby Steps

A nice white shoe
all tied up tight.
Another shoe
all tied just right.
Time to try it.

Time to see
if baby wants
to walk with me.
I'll hold your hands.
I'll hold on tight.

You won't fall down.
You'll be all right.

Take a step.
And then take two.

Look and see
what you can do!

We'll walk this way
and then walk that.

We'll pet the dog
and then the cat.

Baby, I'm so proud of you!
Look and see
what you can do!

Baby Shampoo

A little tub,
a bit of soap,
a bottle of shampoo.
A rub-a-dub,
a soapy scrub,
a baby bath for you!

We'll wash your pretty little feet.
We'll wash your pretty head.

We'll wrap you in a fluffy towel
and dry you on the bed.

You'll smell so sweet.
You'll be so clean.
Your nose will have a glow.

Happy baby.
Squeaky clean!
You know I love you so.

Baby Carriage

Let's go out
and see the world.

First we'll find a bonnet
and your favorite blankie
with the kitty cats all on it.

Find a little sweater
and some socks for little feet.

Here's our carriage.
Here we go.
You just look so sweet!

Feel the sun
and feel the wind
and hear the nice birdsong.

Baby carriage wheels are turning
as we roll along.

Everyone will smile at us.
I think we should smile too.

What a happy day this is.
Baby, I love you.

Baby Teeth

Little teeth are coming in,
nice and white and new.
Baby teeth for chewing things.
Now, what shall you chew?

How about a bit of bun?

How about some toast?

How about some building blocks?
I think you love those most.

If I find a tickle spot,
maybe you will wiggle.

And I'll see your pretty teeth
every time you giggle.

We will count them,
one, two, three.
Maybe even four.

I love your little baby teeth.
I love you even more.

Baby Bed

Sleepy eyes and sleepy head,
baby needs a baby bed.

First some milk
and then some rocking.
I will sing
instead of talking.

Let me hold you
nice and tight.
Let me kiss
your head good night.

Here's a cozy baby bed
for a sleepy baby head.

A favorite bear,
a comfy pup.
A bunting which will
wrap you up.

Sleep, my sweetheart.
Sleep, my dear.
Sleep and sleep.
I'll be right here.